THE TAMING OF THE SHREW

By Jennifer Mulherin   Illustrations by Gwen Green

CHERRYTREE BOOKS

CHERRYTREE BOOKS

Cherrytree Books
50 Godfrey Avenue
Twickenham
TW2 7PF
UK

British Library Cataloguing in Publication Data (CIP) exists for this title.

ISBN   9781842347713
Title   The Taming of the Shrew

Printed in Malta by Melita Press

Author's Note

There is no substitute for seeing the plays of Shakespeare performed. Only then can you really understand why Shakespeare is our greatest dramatist and poet. This book simply gives you the background to the play and tells you about the story and characters. It will, I hope, encourage you to see the play

Visit our website: www.cherrytreebooks.co.uk

The duties of
a wife

This affectionate portrait of the painter Peter Paul Rubens with his wife, dated around 1609, shows that men and women believed in love within marriage, then as now.

At the end of *The Taming of the Shrew*, Kate, the heroine, makes a long speech in which she submits to her husband's will and promises to obey him. Unlike modern people, Shakespeare's audience would not have been at all troubled by this submissiveness. In those times, wives were expected to bow to their husband's authority. This is not to say that women were oppressed, or that decisions were not made jointly. But in family and household matters – should there be disagreements – the husband's decision was final. The Elizabethans believed in a divinely ordered scheme of things descending from God down to all the creatures on earth. Within this, everyone had their place – so servants were the subjects of their masters, and wives inferior to their husbands.

The Tudor household

Although the husband and father had absolute authority within the family, his task was not easy. He was responsible for providing all the material comforts for his wife and family. This included looking after elderly or dependent relatives.

In grander households, he had to employ a tutor or domestic chaplain for his children's education. Any servants or retainers had to be housed and fed. Also, like Kate's father, he had to negotiate the marriages of his children. Marriage contracts were common in Tudor times, especially when property and possessions were at stake.

Daily tasks

In return for the security offered by her husband, the Elizabethan wife was responsible for the efficient and thrifty running of his household. This involved the planning and preparation of meals, and organizing servants such as the cook, nurse and maids to do their daily tasks. In addition, a wife presided over the stillroom. This was the place where herbs, flowers and spices were kept and dried to make the home remedies for minor illnesses. Here she also made the fragrant preparations which perfumed linens and repelled pests.

A wife's special responsibility was the care and education of her children. In Elizabethan times, many children died in infancy or from common childhood illnesses. Home remedies or preparations from apothecaries were used to treat them. A mother's constant care, however, was just as important. This painting of 1596 by Marcus Gheeraerts the Younger shows Lady Sidney with five of her children, all dressed as miniature adults, as was the custom.

4

The ingredients came from the kitchen garden, the planting of which a wife also supervised. The stillroom book, where the recipes for such preparations were recorded, was kept by the lady of the house herself and handed down to her daughters.

Here a father presides over prayers and Bible readings in the home. Family prayers, led by the head of house, were part of the daily ritual in Elizabethan times. In large households, family members and servants could be fined for non-attendance. One wifely duty was to supervise the religious instruction of younger children.

Care of the children

In an age when many children died in infancy, a mother was particularly concerned for her children. She personally nursed them when they were ill. Often, she also taught them how to read and write, and daughters were carefully tutored in the art of housekeeping. Book-keeping and domestic skills would be necessary for them in later life.

Harmony in the home

These were only a few of a wife's duties. Above all, she had to make sure that harmony reigned within the home. This meant dealing with any unexpected crisis that might arise. In fact, the well-being of every member of the household – from the humblest serving maid to her husband – was in her hands, so she needed both wisdom and tact. Not all Elizabethan women made good wives, but it was an ideal to live up to.

Right: The painting shows the first meeting of Kate and Petruchio. It is clear from her expression that she is not at all responsive to the cheerful and teasing words with which Petruchio greets her.

6

A sexist play?

On stage and on screen, this is a very successful and funny play. Its theme – marriage and the role of women – has always made it popular. It is full of high jinks and action, and audiences simply go along with its knockabout style. The disguises and mistakes which are part of the plot are effective on stage, although they often make tedious reading.

In the 20th century, *The Taming of the Shrew* was made into a musical called *Kiss Me Kate*, with words and music by Cole Porter. The play has been filmed 11 times; the most lively and popular version, which is still available on video, is the 1966 movie by Franco Zeffirelli starring Elizabeth Taylor and Richard Burton. It has also been produced for television several times.

A play within a play

The story of the 'taming of the shrew' is a play within a play. It is performed by a troupe of travelling actors in a nobleman's house. 'Strolling players' were common in Tudor times. They travelled the country, setting up a stage and scenery at country fairs and festivals to perform a play for the crowds. And, as here, they often played in noblemen's houses. They usually had a small repertoire of plays and would choose one suitable for the occasion.

The play within a play was often used as a device by playwrights. Shakespeare, for instance, has a troupe of actors in *Hamlet*, who perform a short play. In *The Taming of the Shrew*, though, Shakespeare seems to lose interest in the story of the drunken tinker Sly, and does not return to it at the end of the shrew story. It is perhaps for this reason that the opening *Induction* scenes are left out of many modern productions of the play.

Nagging wives

Stories about nagging or unruly wives were popular well before and even after Shakespeare's time, and they appear in many old ballads and folk tales. Usually, in the old tales, the husband triumphs over his wife by using brute force, as in the Punch and Judy puppet shows of a slightly later age. Shakespeare does not take this line.

Strolling players travelled about the country, carrying with them the scenery, costumes, musical instruments and other paraphernalia needed for their performances.

What happens in the play is that, in the end, Kate submits to her husband by choice – not force.

Modern disapproval

Many people today feel uncomfortable about *The Shrew* because it seems to be about the tyranny of man over woman. They regard it as a 'sexist play' and say that Kate is demeaned by her husband. One theatre critic has said that the play is 'totally offensive to our age and society' and that it should be 'put back firmly and squarely on the shelf'. This, you may think, misses the point.

Firstly, the Elizabethans did not believe in the equality of the sexes as we do. For them, it was a God-given right

In this famous scene from the play (Act 4, Scene 1), an enraged Petruchio throws the food and dishes at the servants, insulting them and shouting that the meat is overcooked. Kate tries unsuccessfully to calm him.

for a husband to dominate his wife in all things, just as a king could dictate to his subjects, or a human being control an animal.

Christian beliefs

At the end of the play, Kate emphasizes a wife's duty 'to serve, love and obey'. Here she is clearly referring to the words that were part of the Church of England marriage service until fairly recent times, and are still chosen by some couples. During this, the priest says to the woman, 'Wilt thou obey him, and serve him, love, honour and keep him in sickness and in health?' The *New Testament* also states: 'Wives, submit yourselves unto your husbands, as unto the Lord. For the husband is the head of the wife, even as Christ is the head of the church.' The Elizabethans had strong Christian beliefs, and followed the teachings of the Church. Kate is merely giving voice to ideas that were accepted by everyone in Shakespeare's day.

Secondly, the play is a moving story of love and commitment, the very basis of marriage, then as now. At the beginning of the play, Kate is a stubborn and difficult woman. Petruchio wants to curb her wilfulness. He does this very cleverly by throwing tantrums and behaving irrationally – much as Kate does herself. She finally gives in to him and becomes a conventional wife. This is because she has seen in Petruchio's actions the ugliness of her own behaviour.

Her submission is moving because it is so genuine. With his help, she has learned self-control and how to care about someone other than herself. The actress Meryl Streep emphasized this aspect of the play when she played Kate in 1978 and said, 'What I'm saying is, I'll do anything for this man . . . Why is selflessness wrong here? Service is the only thing that's important about love'.

The story of
The Taming of the Shrew

Outside an alehouse in Warwickshire a tinker, Christopher Sly, falls into a drunken sleep. A nobleman and his hunting party approach the inn.

Playing a trick

The lord sees the sleeping Sly and decides to play a trick on him. He asks his servants to take the drunkard to his home. When Sly awakes, everyone is to pretend that he is really a nobleman who has been sick and out of his mind.

A troupe of actors with a play

Sly is carried off and a company of actors arrives. The nobleman welcomes them and asks them to perform a play before the 'lord' (Sly). When the tinker wakes up, he protests that he is not a lord. After some persuasion, he grows accustomed to his new role. He settles down to watch the play, which is *The Taming of the Shrew*.

In Padua, Italy

Lucentio, a young man from Pisa, arrives in Padua with his manservant Tranio. They encounter Baptista, a wealthy gentleman with two daughters, Bianca and Katherina. Bianca is sweet and kind, but the elder daughter Katherina is bad-tempered and shrewish. Baptista insists that a husband must be found for Kate before he will allow Bianca to marry.

Bianca's suitors

Bianca's two suitors, Hortensio and Gremio, are joined by Lucentio, who has fallen in love with Bianca at first sight. He decides to change places with Tranio so that, by offering his services as a tutor, he can be close to Bianca and win her love. Tranio meanwhile pretends to be Lucentio.

With his servant Grumio, Petruchio arrives in Padua to visit his friend Hortensio. Petruchio wants to find a wife in Padua, preferably a rich one; he plans to marry, and 'if wealthily, then happily', he declares. When he hears about Katherina, he decides that she is the wife for him.

Petruchio decides to woo the shrew

While they talk, Hortensio and Petruchio are joined by Gremio and Lucentio, disguised as a schoolmaster. They

are joined by a third suitor, who calls himself Lucentio (this is Tranio in disguise). Petruchio explains his decision to woo Katherina. He is not put off by her shrewish reputation. In fact, he regards wooing her as a challenge.

Petruchio takes up the challenge
Think you a little din can daunt mine ears?
Have I not in my time heard lions roar?
Have I not heard the sea, puffed up with winds,
Rage like an angry boar chafed with sweat?
... And do you tell me of a woman's tongue,
That gives not half so great a blow to hear
As will a chestnut in a farmer's fire?

Act I Sc ii

Introducing Bianca and Katherina

In Baptista's house, Bianca and Katherina are quarrelling. Kate shows her ill nature by striking her gentle sister. At this moment, Petruchio, Gremio, Lucentio (disguised as a tutor), Hortensio (also disguised, but as a musician) and 'Lucentio' (Tranio) come to see Baptista.

Petruchio asks for Katherina's hand in marriage. Baptista is incredulous, but Petruchio convinces him that he is in earnest. He can be as rough and as headstrong as she is, he declares. Kate and Petruchio then meet, and immediately begin to trade insults.

15

Kate responds to Petruchio's sarcasm by striking him but he does not react. He teases her, saying she is gentle and courteous. He says he is determined to marry her, and that he will change her from a wild, stubborn creature to a more 'conformable' one.

When her father and the others appear, Kate berates her father for wanting her to marry Petruchio. But Petruchio declares that they are to be married the following Sunday. Although Kate says she'll see him 'hanged on Sunday first', Petruchio assures them that she has agreed to the marriage, but is simply keeping up her shrewish front in public.

The highest bidder

Now that the marriage of Katherina has been arranged, Bianca's suitors ask Baptista for her hand. Tranio (as Lucentio) and Gremio both boast of their wealth – for Baptista has said that the highest bidder wins his younger daughter. Tranio, declaring he is the owner of several homes, much land and a fleet of merchant ships, wins the bid. However, it seems that this wealth belongs to his father and Bianca might be left penniless if he were to die young. Baptista agrees to the marriage of Tranio/Lucentio, but only on condition that Lucentio's father agrees to support his son's pledge. Meanwhile, Petruchio goes off to Venice to buy the rings and fine clothing for his wedding.

In the classroom

Bianca's most ardent suitors – Lucentio disguised as a schoolmaster and Hortensio as a musician – present themselves to her as tutors. They exchange cross words about who is to spend more time with her, but she rebukes them, saying she will decide how she learns her lessons. She instructs Hortensio to play the lute while she has a lesson in Latin grammar from Lucentio.

Kate rebukes her father
Call you me 'daughter'?
Now I promise you
You have shown a tender
fatherly regard,
To wish me wed to one
half-lunatic,
A madcap ruffian and a
swearing Jack,
That thinks with oaths
to face the matter out.

Act II Sc i

16

Conquering Kate

Thou must be married to no man but me.
For I am he am born to tame you, Kate,
And bring you from a wild Kate to a Kate
Conformable as other household Kates.

Act II Sc i

The Latin lesson proceeds, despite interruptions from Hortensio. Lucentio, sitting close to Bianca, tells her his true identity and that he has come to woo her.

A Latin lesson

I am Lucentio; 'hic est', *son unto Vincentio of Pisa;* 'Sigeia tellus', *disguised thus to get your love;* 'Hic steterat', *and that Lucentio that comes a-wooing;* 'Priami', *is my man Tranio;* 'regia', *bearing my port;* 'celsa senis', *that we might beguile the old pantaloon.*

Act III Sc i

Bianca's response

Bianca is a little wary of this declaration, and she responds cautiously but favourably. 'I know you not,' she says. 'I trust you not . . . take heed he hear us not . . . despair not,' she whispers.

Hortensio watches this exchange and is somewhat peeved that Lucentio 'doth court my love'. But Bianca now agrees to have her music lesson, and it is Lucentio's turn to watch while Hortensio whispers words of passionate love. She is not particularly impressed by these, and at that moment is called away to prepare for her sister's wedding day. Hortensio suspects that his cause may be lost, and mutters that he may have to find another love.

Waiting for the bridegroom
All is prepared for the wedding of Kate and Petruchio but Baptista, along with his daughters and Bianca's suitors, awaits the arrival of Petruchio, who is late.

Baptista voices his shame and embarrassment at his absence. 'What mockery will it be To want the bridegroom when the priest attends?' he asks.

Kate says that the shame is hers, and that she should never have agreed to marry Petruchio. She bursts into tears.

Kate's shame

He'll woo a thousand, 'point the day of marriage,
Make feast, invite friends and proclaim the banns,
Yet never means to wed where he hath wooed.
Now must the world point at poor Katherine,
And say, 'Lo, there is mad Petruchio's wife,
If it would please him come and marry her'.

Act III Sc ii

19

Petruchio's appearance

Why, Petruchio is coming in a new hat and an old jerkin; a pair of old breeches thrice turned; a pair of boots that have been candle-cases, one buckled, another laced; an old rusty sword . . . with a broken hilt . . . his horse hipped, with an old mothy saddle and stirrups of no kindred;

Act III Sc ii

Petruchio's arrival

At that moment, Baptista's servant announces that Petruchio has arrived with his manservant. He goes on to describe his astonishing appearance. Petruchio wears tattered clothing, carries a rusty sword and rides a lame, sick horse.

Baptista is naturally appalled that his future son-in-law should be so ill-dressed, but Petruchio protests that Katherina is marrying the man, not the clothes. Things do not go well at the church, either. Petruchio stamps his foot and swears at the priest, who drops the prayer-book. He then calls for wine and, after drinking it, throws the dregs at the sexton. The marriage over, he kisses the bride and sweeps out of the church.

> **A mad marriage**
> *. . . he took the bride about the neck,*
> *And kissed her lips with such a clamorous smack*
> *That at the parting all the church did echo . . .*
> *Such a mad marriage never was before.*
>
> Act III Sc ii

Baptista has, of course, arranged a wedding feast, but Petruchio refuses to stay for this. Despite entreaties and his wife's protestations, he insists on taking her away, while the guests

21

remain to enjoy the wedding banquet. Petruchio dares anyone to stop him, saying that now Kate is his wife, she must do as he wishes.

> **Petruchio asserts his rights**
> *I will be master of what is mine own.*
> *She is my goods, my chattels, she is my house,*
> *My household stuff, my field, my barn,*
> *My horse, my ox, my ass, my any thing,*
> *And here she stands, touch her whoever dare!*

Act III Sc ii

Turbulent times

On the journey from Padua, Petruchio sets out to outdo Kate by behaving even more outrageously than she ever did. He shouts, curses and insults a servant for spilling a little water. When food is served, Petruchio sends it away, declaring it is overcooked. Kate protests and defends the servants; she asks her husband to show patience and forgiveness but, alas, he will not listen. Worse still, he prevents her from sleeping by throwing off the sheets and bed covers, saying that the bed was not properly made. 'Ay, and amid this hurly I intend That all is done in reverent care of her . . . This is the way to kill a wife with kindness,' says Petruchio. In fact, these antics are part of his plan to 'tame' Kate little by little, as he would a falcon.

Bianca's choice

Meanwhile, back in Padua, Bianca has fallen in love with the schoolmaster Lucentio. Hortensio withdraws as her suitor and announces he is going to marry a rich widow. Tranio, however, has to keep up the pretence of being the Lucentio (subject to a pledge from his father) who

has Baptista's approval for Bianca's hand in marriage. Tranio finds a passing traveller who agrees to act as Lucentio's father and pledge the financial support demanded earlier by Baptista.

At his house, Petruchio continues his taming of Katherina. He has ordered a cap and a fine gown for his wife, but again rejects them as unfit to wear. Kate protests but to no avail. Petruchio announces that they will return to her father's house in their shabby clothes, since appearances do not matter.

Petruchio on appearances
Our purses shall be proud, our garments poor,
For 'tis the mind that makes the body rich;
And as the sun breaks through the darkest clouds,
So honour peereth in the meanest habit.
What, is the jay more precious than the lark
Because his feathers are more beautiful?
Or is the adder better than the eel
Because his painted skin contents the eye?

Act IV Sc iii

23

An elopement

Back in Padua, the pretend Lucentio and his pretend father discuss the marriage settlement for Bianca. While this is happening, the real Lucentio and Bianca go off to a church, where a priest awaits to marry them.

The journey to Padua

Petruchio and Katherina have started their journey back to Padua. Although they argue about the time of day, Kate has become less difficult. She finally gives up contradicting her husband after they meet an old man on the road, who turns out to be Vincentio, Lucentio's real father. He is on his way to Padua to visit his son. Petruchio declares that the man is a 'fair lovely maid' and orders Kate to greet him as such. When she does, her husband corrects her. She then apologizes to Vincentio for her mistake. Petruchio has at last won the 'battle of the sexes'.

Kate gives in

Pardon, old father, my mistaking eyes
That have been so bedazzled with the sun
That everything I look on seemeth green.
Now I perceive thou art a reverend father;
Pardon, I pray thee, for my mad mistaking.

Act IV Sc v

The false identities revealed

In Padua, Bianca and Lucentio have been married. When Petruchio, Kate and Vincentio arrive, they argue with Tranio's fake father, who still maintains the pretence with Baptista. With the arrival of Lucentio and Bianca, the false identities are revealed, and all is well.

A marriage feast

Everyone is gathered for a banquet to celebrate the marriages of the three couples – Katherina and Petruchio, Bianca and Lucentio, and Hortensio, who has married his rich widow.

To convince the company that Kate is no longer a shrew, Petruchio proposes a wager. When the three women leave the room, each husband will call for his wife. The first wife to respond by coming straight away will win the bet.

Both Hortensio and Lucentio ask for their wives, but they reply that they are busy and cannot come. When Petruchio calls for Kate, she comes at once and asks, 'What is your will, sir . . . ?' Kate has won the bet for Petruchio. She then gives the other wives a lecture on a woman's duty to her husband.

A woman's place

Kate chides the women for being scornful and wounding. They should obey their husbands. 'Such duty as the subject owes the prince, Even such, a woman oweth to her husband,' she declares. She points out that husbands care for their wives, and look after them by working to support them. When women are 'peevish, sullen, sour', they are a 'graceless traitor' to their loving lord, she adds. Kate, it seems, speaks sincerely from her own experience and feelings. Then, in a sudden gesture of submission and gratitude, she places her hand beneath Petruchio's foot.

Her husband is so touched by Kate's generosity and love that he can think of nothing to say except, 'Why, there's a wench! Come on, and kiss me, Kate.'

Kate's view of marriage

Thy husband is thy lord, thy life, thy keeper,
Thy head, thy sovereign: one that cares for thee,
And for thy maintenance; commits his body
To painful labour both by sea and land,
To watch the night in storms, the day in cold,
Whilst thou liest warm at home, secure and safe,
And craves no other tribute at thy hands
But love, fair looks, and true obedience –
Too little payment for so great a debt.

Act v Sc ii

Love, not war

I am ashamed that women are so simple
To offer war where they should kneel for peace;
Or seek for rule, supremacy, and sway
When they are bound to serve, love, and obey.
Why are our bodies soft, and weak, and smooth,
Unapt to toil and trouble in the world
But that our soft conditions, and our hearts,
Should well agree with our external parts?

Act v Sc ii

The play's characters

Petruchio

Katherina

Petruchio

Petruchio is like many young Elizabethan gentlemen that Shakespeare would have known. He is genial and self-confident, and enjoys good company. But Petruchio is also witty and wise, and his deep understanding of human nature shows through in the way he deals with Kate. Even when he behaves badly himself, with no concern for others and criticizing everything, he is caring and good-humoured with his wife. He understands the reason for Kate's bad temper. She has, after all, always been compared unfavourably with her sister, and is defensive. By his own example, he cunningly shows her how unattractive her behaviour is. Under his guidance, she becomes a different person. During the course of the play, Petruchio falls in love with Kate, and calls her 'sweet Kate' when they touchingly exchange a kiss before the wedding banquet. At the end of the play, his response to her speech on the duties of a wife is absolute delight. He is full of pride and love for his wife.

Petruchio's ambition

I come to wive it wealthily in Padua;
If wealthily, then happily in Padua.

Act I Sc ii

28

Katherina

At the beginning of the play, Katherina is a bad-tempered young woman, who is compared unkindly to her gentle sister Bianca. She has a reputation as a shrew, and certainly she is rude and insulting to everyone she encounters. She even goes so far as to hit her music teacher with a lute and to slap both Bianca and Petruchio. She is shunned by everyone, except Petruchio. He sees that she is not much loved by her sister and father, which is probably the reason for her behaviour. Kate accepts Petruchio's control because, by being calm and submissive, she finds happiness. Some readers are appalled by this. They think she is an oppressed person dominated by a selfish man. But this view is based on modern ideas about marriage. In Shakespeare's day, wives did defer to their husbands. Kate certainly loves her husband. They talk affectionately to each other, and she calls him 'love'. Shakespeare clearly believed in loving marriages. He also believed in the idea of unselfishness and service in a wife.

Baptista

The father of Katherina and Bianca, Baptista is an elderly, rich man. He clearly prefers his younger daughter to Kate, and rarely has a good word to say for Kate. Once she is betrothed,

Baptista

Kate's reputation

Her name is Katherina Minola,
Renowned in Padua for her scolding tongue.

Act I Sc ii

Baptista's marriage terms for Kate

Ay, when the special thing is well obtained,
That is, her love; for that is all in all.

Act I Sc ii

Lucentio

Women had no means of support other than their family or husbands. Marriage was as much a business deal as a love match, and marriage settlements were common among well-off families in Elizabethan times.

Bianca

Kate's sister, Bianca, is beautiful and demure. However, she is not quite as sweet as she seems at first. She is catty about Kate's age, and when left alone with her tutors she is quite petulant. She flirts with the schoolmaster Lucentio and sharply rejects her other suitor Hortensio. Finally, she ridicules her husband, Lucentio, for making a bet on her wifely duty. Shakespeare leaves us wondering if this couple will be as happy as Kate and Petruchio.

Lucentio

Lucentio is a romantic young man smitten with love for Bianca. He does not understand her very well. This is probably because he is too love-sick to see any faults in her. Love also makes him impetuous. He elopes with her, instead of courting her openly. However, at the end of the play, he finds Bianca is not quite as demure as he thought.

Lucentio in love
. . . I burn, I pine, I perish . . .
If I achieve not this young
*   modest girl.*

Act I Sc i

Bianca

he auctions Bianca to the highest bidder. This may seem shocking but Baptista's concern that his daughters should be financially secure was natural. When Petruchio asks for Katherina's hand in marriage, Baptista does insist that Petruchio must win her love.

Lucentio on Bianca
. . . I saw her coral lips to move,
And with her breath she did perfume the air.
Sacred and sweet was all I saw in her.

Act I Sc i

The life and plays of Shakespeare

Life of Shakespeare

1564 William Shakespeare born at Stratford-upon-Avon.

1582 Shakespeare marries Anne Hathaway, eight years his senior.

1583 Shakespeare's daughter, Susanna, is born.

1585 The twins, Hamnet and Judith, are born.

1587 Shakespeare goes to London.

1591-2 Shakespeare writes *The Comedy of Errors*. He is becoming well-known as an actor and writer.

1592 Theatres closed because of plague.

1593-4 Shakespeare writes *Titus Andronicus* and *The Taming of the Shrew*: he is a member of the theatrical company, the Chamberlain's Men.

1594-5 Shakespeare writes *Romeo and Juliet*.

1595 Shakespeare writes *A Midsummer Night's Dream*.

1595-6 Shakespeare writes *Richard II*.

1596 Shakespeare's son, Hamnet, dies. Shakespeare writes *King John* and *The Merchant of Venice*.

1597 Shakespeare buys New Place in Stratford.

1597-8 Shakespeare writes *Henry IV*.

1599 Shakespeare's theatre company opens the Globe Theatre.

1599-1600 Shakespeare writes *As You Like It, Henry V* and *Twelfth Night*.

1600-01 Shakespeare writes *Hamlet*.

1602-03 Shakespeare writes *All's Well That Ends Well*.

1603 Elizabeth I dies. James I becomes king. Theatres closed because of plague.

1603-04 Shakespeare writes *Othello*.

1605 Theatres closed because of plague.

1605-06 Shakespeare writes *Macbeth* and *King Lear*.

1606-07 Shakespeare writes *Antony and Cleopatra*.

1607 Susanna Shakespeare marries Dr John Hall. Theatres closed because of plague.

1608 Shakespeare's granddaughter, Elizabeth Hall, is born.

1609 *Sonnets* published. Theatres closed because of plague.

1610 Theatres closed because of plague. Shakespeare gives up his London lodgings and retires to Stratford.

1611-12 Shakespeare writes *The Tempest*.

1613 Globe Theatre burns to the ground during a performance of *Henry VIII*.

1616 Shakespeare dies on 23 April.

Shakespeare's plays
The Comedy of Errors
Love's Labour's Lost
Henry VI Part 2
Henry VI Part 3
Henry VI Part 1
Richard III
Titus Andronicus
The Taming of the Shrew
The Two Gentlemen of Verona
Romeo and Juliet
Richard II
A Midsummer Night's Dream
King John
The Merchant of Venice
Henry IV Part 1
Henry IV Part 2
Much Ado About Nothing
Henry V
Julius Caesar
As You Like It
Twelfth Night
Hamlet
The Merry Wives of Windsor
Troilus and Cressida
All's Well That Ends Well
Othello
Measure for Measure
King Lear
Macbeth
Antony and Cleopatra
Timon of Athens
Coriolanus
Pericles
Cymbeline
The Winter's Tale
The Tempest
Henry VIII

Index

Picture credits
p. 3 Bridgeman Art Library; p. 5 Reproduced by kind permission of Viscount De L'Isle, from his private collection; p. 7 Bridgeman Art Library; pps. 10-11 Bridgeman Art Library